Peppa's First Sleepover

Peppa is going to her very first sleepover at Zoe Zebra's house. "Welcome to my sleepover!" Zoe says.

"I'll pick you up in the morning," Mummy Pig
says to Peppa with a kiss.

Rebecca Rabbit, Suzy Sheep and
Emily Elephant are already here.
"I've got my teddy," Peppa says.

Zoe has her monkey. Rebecca has her carrot.
Suzy has her owl. And Emily has her frog.

"Don't stay up too late, girls! And don't be too loud.
Daddy Zebra has to get up early to deliver the post,"
Mummy Zebra says as she turns out the lights.

Zoe's baby twin sisters, Zuzu and Zaza,
want to join the sleepover too.
"Sleepovers are only for big girls!" Zoe says.

The twins begin to cry.
"They're so sweet and little," Peppa says.

"Can they stay?" Rebecca asks.
"Okay," Zoe says to the twins.
"But you must NOT fall asleep."

"What should we do first?"
Suzy asks.
"I'm having piano lessons!
Listen . . ." Zoe starts to pound
on the keys. "Twinkle, twinkle,
little star . . ."

Mummy Zebra has woken up,
"Shush! You must be quiet so Daddy Zebra can sleep!
Now, into your sleeping bags please."

"Snort! What do we do now?" Peppa asks.
"At sleepovers, there's always
a midnight feast!" Zoe says.
"It's when we eat things," Suzy says
in a hushed voice. "In secret."

"Shh!" Zoe says as she leads the girls to the kitchen. They each grab some delicious fruit, perfect for a midnight feast. The floorboard creaks.

Oh no! Mummy Zebra has woken up. "You'll wake Daddy Zebra! Now, who knows a bedtime story?"

The girls take turns: "Once upon a time, there was a little fairy . . ." Suzy begins.

"And she lived in the forest . . ." Peppa continues.
"And the fairy met a big monster, who went . . .
RAARRR!" Emily says with a big
elephant trumpet noise!

Oh dear. The noise has woken Daddy Zebra!
"Sorry, Daddy," Zoe says. "There was a story
about a fairy and a scary monster."

"And we want to know what happens next!" Peppa says.
"Very well," Daddy Zebra sighs. "The monster lifted up
his great, big hairy paws . . ."

"And walked along on his great, big hairy feet . . . And sang . . . 'Twinkle, twinkle little star how I wonder what you are . . .'" Daddy Zebra sings gently as he plays the piano.

Daddy Zebra's song has
sent everyone to sleep.

Collect these other great Peppa Pig stories